The First Date Disaster

A Very Merry Murder Mystery, Volume 2

Rachel Beattie

Published by Rachel Beattie, 2024.

THE FIRST DATE DISASTER

First edition. May 3, 2024.

Copyright © 2024 Rachel Beattie.

ISBN: 979-8224093953

Written by Rachel Beattie.

Chapter One

"Honestly, Snuffy. Anyone would think your life was in danger."

I try to whisper, but my voice carries further than I mean it to, and over the constant yowling from inside my cat-carrier I lock eyes with another pet owner who laughs.

"Not a fan of veterinary practice waiting rooms?"

"Me or the cat?" I joke, before another perfectly-timed howl.

My neighbor's pet - a chocolate labrador snoring contentedly at her feet - is much better behaved. I smile.

"Whoever told me cats were quieter than dogs lied."

"Oh, this one can make plenty of noise when she wants to." She leans down and scratches the dog behind her ear and she obediently rolls over, demanding belly rubs. "She used to be a nightmare to bring to her vet appointments, but ever since Dr. Castle started here she's been so much better behaved." Her eyes sparkle with amusement. "We all behave ourselves when Dr. Castle's around."

My cheeks flood with heat and I drop my gaze. My reasons for being here are purely professional. I've owned Snuffy the cat long enough that he's come due for his next round of vaccinations, and being the responsible new-pet-owner I now am, I booked him in for a check-up. So what if I asked for Dr. Rob Castle by name and willingly took an awkward, middle-of-the-morning slot to specifically see him?

A door opens and a handsome blond head appears, attached to a body that has no right to be as tall and broad-shouldered as it is.

"Good morning, Merry! And I assume that -" He winces as Snuffy hits a particularly high note. "Is my eleven o'clock?"

"Certainly is," I say, jumping to my feet and reaching for the cat carrier. Motion seems to only make Snuffy even more vocal, and as my waiting-room neighbor waves to me, I swear her dog lets out a sigh of relief that the source of the noise will soon be safely locked away behind a very thick door.

"Alright, let's see what we have here..." Rob squints into a tablet and then looks up at me. "Shots?

I nod, then fumble with the catch on the cat-carrier.

"Oh, wait a second -"

The plastic door is open before I have time to react, and Snuffy suddenly becomes part-ninja, diving through the gap between my hands and Rob's as he makes for the door. It's closed, but that only seems to faze him for half a second. He darts through my legs and scrambles into a corner, hissing and crying like he's trapped in a room with a sadist. I glance at Rob, who scoops him up like this is nothing out of the ordinary.

"Here." He passes him to me. "Go to Mommy."

Mommy? I've never completely understood those people who dote on their fur-babies more than their actual babies, but somehow I end up rocking Snuffy like he's a newborn and wouldn't you know it, it works. He stops crying and apart from digging his claws into my forearm she seems much more at ease.

"Can you keep hold of him? It's probably easier to do it this way." Rob lifts a syringe filled with a clear liquid and leans over me, pinching Snuffy on the back of his neck and swiftly administering the shot. His head is bent so close to mine that I can smell his cologne and my eyes flutter closed. "There, all done." I blink and he's looking at me, his eyes crinkling at the corners in amusement. "This is your first time bringing him in, isn't it?"

I nod and try to ease two sets of very sharp claws out of the flesh of my forearm.

"Don't worry. It gets easier." Rob pats me gently on the shoulder, then offers Snuffy a treat he's pulled out of thin air.

"Maybe for you," I say, taking advantage of my cat's interest in the treat to manhandle him back into the carrier. I turn the latch, making sure he's safely trapped in there, and examine the damage, poking at the claw marks in my arm, several of which have drawn blood.

"Ouch!" Rob turns away from me for a moment, rummaging in a drawer before emerging with a disinfectant wipe he holds out to me. "Here. Allow me." Tearing open the top, he unfolds the thin tissue and wipes it carefully over the scratches on my arm making me flinch. *Holy hell, that hurts.* "Very good. You're the second-best patient I've treated in the last five minutes." He winks at me. "No treat for you, though, I'm afraid."

Damnit. I never can tell if Rob's just being friendly or actually flirting. It's thanks to him I even have this ridiculous cat to begin with, after he helped me accidentally solve a murder and left me the only viable option of a forever home for my furry new best buddy. It was perfect timing, too, as I was just about getting used to living on my own after finalizing my divorce. Since then, Snuffy and I have been mostly inseparable. I press my free hand against the stinging scratches on my forearm and wish that today we hadn't been quite *so* inseparable.

"How's Snuffy getting along otherwise? Eating ok? Sleeping? Exercising?"

"Fine." I count off my answers to his questions on my fingers. "Yes, everything he can find. All day, every day, and only when he has to. Or the middle of the night, when I'm trying to sleep."

"Excellent. He's a textbook cat, then," he says, as the chorus of complaining starts up again, lower in volume but no less miserable than before. "And you're enjoying being a pet owner?"

"Beats having a houseplant for company." I grimace. That makes me sound like some sort of antisocial loon. "I mean, yeah. It's great. He's great."

"Great."

We're standing there staring at each other for a moment, and I'm just thinking there's nothing that can make this moment better when he says my name.

"Meredith?"

"Rob." I look up at him through soft lashes and think - this is it. This is the moment all our maybe-might-be flirting is going to lead to him asking me out on an actual date.

"Is there anything else I can help you with today?"

My non-romantical dreams come crashing down around me and Snuffy finds another pitch to wail in stereo about my stupidity. I can feel my cheeks flash hot and red and I force myself to smile.

"No," I say, faintly willing more lightness into my voice than I feel. "No, that's everything. Thank you."

"Thank *you*." He pours hand sanitizer into his palm and works it over both hands. "You can pay at reception and book Snuffy's next checkup for twelve months. They'll probably want to give you a course of flea and worm treatment too. And if there's anything before that, you know where to find me."

"I certainly do!" I turn away, rolling my eyes at my fake cheerfulness. Grabbing Snuffy's cat carrier by its handle I reach for the door and ease my way around it and into the waiting room, right into the middle of an argument.

"There! See! He's not busy now. Dr. Castle! Dr. Castle! Please! You have to help me! It's an emergency!"

The word *emergency* isn't so much a sob as it is a shriek, and it's enough to make Rob follow me out of the examination room and into the waiting room where a woman is tugging on the collar of a very excitable-looking spaniel. The woman might be panicking but the dog is showing no signs of distress at all. He seems to think this is a fun game, and every time the woman tries to tug on his collar to make him move, he inches lower to the ground until he's lying flat, his tail wagging furiously against the linoleum.

"Ms. Davis, you'll have to wait your turn. I'm afraid Dr. Castle has other patients to see..."

"It's fine, Jenny." I feel a warm hand on my back as Rob steps around me and makes his way towards the dog, squatting down and reaching out to pet him. "What seems to be the problem, huh?"

"He swallowed them."

"Hmm?" Rob looks up from his quick examination of the dog's eyes, ears, and teeth and I can see the concern flicker in a shadow across his face. "What did he swallow? When?"

"This morning! About thirty minutes ago! My boyfriend's priceless diamond cufflinks!"

I'm barely conscious of moving as I watch this little soap opera play out, but my knee nudges against a chair and it squeaks against the linoleum. I look away just long enough to rest

Snuffy's cat carrier on the empty seat and keep watching, wondering just what's going to happen next.

"Cufflinks."

"Cufflinks!" The woman nods. "They're very expensive!"

"Ok, let's see." Rob opens the dog's mouth gently, angling the poor thing's head this way and that to see if there's any trace of the cufflinks but evidently not. "And he definitely swallowed them?"

"He must have done! They aren't anywhere else!"

"Ok, boy." Rob runs a hand down the dog's back, patting him gently as he goes. "How's he been since then? Any choking or sickness? And in general, is he quite healthy? Any allergies?"

"I don't know." The woman frowns. "I'm only watching him for a couple of days. No, I don't think so."

"Ok, good." Rob takes a breath. "So you think he swallowed a pair of cufflinks. How big were they?"

"What?"

"The cufflinks. How big? Any sharp edges? Anything that might break or come loose?" Rob's speaking patiently but I get the feeling his concern is more for the dog than his owner, who seems more worried about her boyfriend's lost property than the damage they might cause the poor pooch.

"I just want them back. Can't you make him throw up or something?"

"We could try an emetic," Rob says, still stroking the dog. "We should probably do a scan to find out where they are. Can you get me a picture of these cufflinks? And tell me roughly how big they are. Come on, boy. Let's take you through and have a proper look at you...." He lifts his head expectantly, but the woman is furiously tapping away at her phone and misses the gesture.

"We'll need to take some details." The secretary, Jenny, is sharp, but not unkind. "Your dog's name is...?"

"Here." Ignoring the question, the woman turns her phone around, pointing the screen at Rob. "You see? They're very expensive."

"I see." Rob scoops up the dog, who wriggles as he's lifted, and together they stroll swiftly into the empty examination room. I hear the whisper of Rob's voice as the door swings closed behind them. "Come on, boy. Let's get you sorted out..."

The woman doesn't follow them. She doesn't even seem to notice they've gone. She's tapping away on her phone again until Rob's secretary clears her throat noisily.

"Can I take some details for our records, Ms. Davis?"

"Charlotte." The woman is still typing. "You can call me Charlotte."

"Charlotte. And what's your dog's name?"

"Oh, he isn't my dog! He's my sister's." She scowls. "She asked me to look after him while she's getting some work done at her house and it's just been one disaster after another. He gets into everything. This isn't the first time he's tried to eat something that belongs to me, you know. I think he must have worms. It's not like I don't feed him. And - "

"The dog's name, Ms. Davis."

"Oh, Brick. As in dumb-as-a." She sniffs. I get the feeling she was trying to make a joke, but there is nothing at all amusing about her tone of voice and the comment lands like a lead weight. I glance at the woman who's sharing the waiting area with me and notice her arms are protectively wrapped around her own dog as if this woman's disdain might be catching. I hug Snuffy's carrier a little closer to me and think what might have happened to the obnoxious little furball if I hadn't been willing to give him a home.

"Look, is this going to take long?" Charlotte Davis says, answering a relentless string of noisy notifications on her phone. "I need to get back to work. Can't you just give him something to make him sick and then we can get going?"

"Dr. Castle will want to do a thorough investigation." The secretary taps a few keys on her keyboard. "You're welcome to go on back into the examination room and be with Brick if you want. I can print out a copy of this form for you to take with you."

Charlotte looks over her shoulder at the doorway as if she's contemplating making a run for it, but in the end, she lets out a long breath and slides her phone into the side pocket of an expensive-looking purse she clutches daintily with one hand. She holds the other out for the form that buzzes hot out of the printer, and stalks after Rob in a cloud of perfumed annoyance. A second of pure silence passes where none of us move or even breathe before the secretary beckons me with a bright, welcoming smile.

"I'm sorry about that, Meredith. Just Snuffy's regular vaccinations, wasn't it? And would you like to book him in for the same again next year?"

Chapter Two

I'm already late when I get out of the clinic, but I still have to take Snuffy home. As soon as the front door closes behind me and I unlatch his carrier he bolts upstairs in a noisy, cat-shaped blur and I don't have time to worry over what sort of chaos-revenge he'll wreak on my house while I'm at work.

Work. I plaster a smile on my face as I hurry back towards Silver Brook's high street and ask myself why I volunteered to take on running the Jitterbug Junction for my friend, Maggie, this week of all weeks.

Because you're a sucker, I tell myself, wincing at what looks like a queue growing ever longer as I dash towards the entrance to the most popular café in town. *Because you can't say no. Because you have nothing close to a career of your own and might as well use your free time for someone else's benefit.*

"Good morning, everyone!" I say, in as cheerful a tone as I can muster. I jangle the keys in a fit of enthusiasm and only manage to elicit a few half-hearted, bad-tempered grumbles in reply. "Thank you for your patience. We'll be up and running again in a snap!" The first key I try won't even fit the lock. The second one fits, but won't turn. I jiggle the handle, but nothing. I resort to going back through the keys one at a time, slowly, and try to ignore the mounting tide of annoyance from my queue of customers.

"It's the big brass one," a nonchalant voice calls from behind me. I turn my head and see an impossibly tall, impossibly young man leaning against the wall. He salutes and then repeats himself. "The key. The brass one." He jerks his thumb at the empty coffee shop. "To open the door?"

"Oh! Right." I turn back to the keys and find what must be *the big brass one* and, wouldn't you know, it fits the lock and turns and everything. The door swings open and I usher my helpful assistant through ahead of me. "You're Gabriel, right?"

"Gabe." His mask of cool slips for half a second as he glances around to check nobody's heard me use his actual Christian name. "Gabe Matthews."

"Glad to meet you, Gabe." I toss him the keys and head straight for the kitchen. "Why don't you open up everything else that needs opening? I'm going to get a jump on the coffee." I'm halfway through pulling on an apron when the front door opens again and I hear the swell and fall of the assembled queue of eager customers. "We aren't open yet - oh." My friendly voice drops as I see one of my oldest friends standing there with his phone out. "What do you want?"

"Photographic proof." Jeremy grins at me and snaps a photo while I'm scrambling to get my apron strings tied. I'm scowling and probably look like some kind of hunchback, but I'm too stressed and tired to tell him off. Instead, I turn around.

"Excellent, well now you have my new dating profile pic sorted can you help me out?"

I can still hear him laughing as he pulls my apron strings tight around my middle, fastening them firmly in a bow.

"So remind me, how long have you been working here?"

"I haven't. Yet." I glance at my watch and yelp, dashing around the Jitterbug's counter and hitting every kind of switch I can find to get things up and running. "Coffee. Where does Maggie keep the coffee?"

"Why are you asking me?" Jeremy slides onto a stool, leaning his elbows on the countertop and watching me lazily.

"Because you're my friend and if you're here right now that means you're going to help me out, right?"

"I'll help you eat one of these peanut butter cookies," he says, glancing down at the glass-covered display of cookies, cakes, and pastries, and even though he isn't looking at me my glare must still hit him because his head shoots up and he smiles. "When you have a minute."

"Alright, Ms. Gray, everything's opened up." Gabe comes back, swinging the keys around his finger. "You want me to let 'em in?"

"Not until you show me where Maggie keeps the coffee!" I say, deciding to let the *Ms. Gray* go for now. Gabe's only a teenager. To him, I probably look as ancient as that title makes me feel.

"What kind?" He grins, and I decide then and there that wrangling teenage boys might be even worse than teenage girls. I'm still recovering from playing *Mama Elf* during this year's Christmas grotto disaster, but it was the aftermath of that - a dead body and a murder investigation - that left Maggie worse off than me and so desperate for a vacation she left me to run her cafe. I glare at Gabe and find it almost as effective on him as it was on Jeremy. "The regular stuff is right here." Placing a palm on the counter he levers himself over and taps a cannister that quite obviously contains coffee beans. I blush, annoyed I didn't spot that. "You grab a measure and grind as required." He makes finger guns towards a medieval torture device that I figure must be the grinder. I shudder. It even *sounds* torturous. "Then there are the specialty blends but...maybe you should let me deal with those, if anyone orders them."

"Good call," I tell him, grabbing an overflowing scoop of coffee beans and spilling half of them on my way to the grinder. "You'd better let everyone in. They've been waiting long enough."

"Didn't Maggie show you how to do any of this?" Jeremy asks me in a low voice, once Gabe's gone to get the door.

"She did." I bite my lip and press a button, hoping for the best and letting out a relieved smile when it noisily whirs into life, grinding my coffee beans into a nice even powder. "But it was very quick and there's a very real chance I wasn't paying attention." I swallow and do my best Maggie impression. "*It's ever so easy, Merry. You'll pick it up in no time. You've been here enough as a customer you practically already know how to run the place! And if there are any problems, you'll have Gabe on hand to help you out...*"

The machine cuts out right at that moment and Gabe turns to look at me, his lips quirking in amusement.

"Did you say my name?"

"I did." I thrust the container of fresh coffee grounds at him. "Why don't you get started making drinks? I need to re-organize the pastry cabinet."

"Sure thing." Gabe takes the coffee and goes to work with all the grace of a concert pianist. I'm sort of mesmerized until Jeremy clears his throat and knocks on the glass front of the cabinet.

"Hmm?"

"Can I get my cookie now?" He grins. "Please?"

"Here." I reach into the glass hatch and lift out the topmost peanut butter cookie and hold it out to him, hesitating with a frown as I slowly begin to piece together a mystery. "Wait, why are you here?"

"I wanted a snack." He eyes the cookie, and I obediently hand it over. "And I wanted to witness the master at work."

Gabe lets out a derisive snort behind me that I choose to ignore, even though I'm privately thanking my lucky stars that, with Maggie gone, he's on hand to help me. I fleetingly wonder if he shouldn't be at school or college or something but there's only enough space in my brain to wonder over one truant at the moment. I fold my arms and glare at Jeremy.

"Why aren't you at work?"

"Day off." He shoves the whole cookie in his mouth at once, his next words muffled by chewing. "And Kate asked me to meet her here."

"Kate's coming?" I groan. I ought to have known that both my best friends could think of nothing better to do today than come and hassle me at my new temporary job. "I suppose I should be grateful that you're at least talking again."

"We're always talking." Jeremy picks a piece of peanut from his teeth and grins. "Sometimes that's in the form of yelling..."

If there's one thing I don't have time or energy to get drawn into today it's the on-again off-again relationship my two best friends have with one another. They recently decided to give dating another shot and for the moment everything is love hearts and candyfloss which I suppose I should be glad about. It certainly makes my life a lot easier when everyone's getting along.

Gabe is progressing swiftly through our line of customers, and I look up at the sound of an annoying - and annoyingly familiar - ringtone that blasts tinnily near the front of the queue. It's Charlotte Davis.

"Good morning!" I wave at her, feigning a friendliness I do not feel. "You were at the vet's this morning, I think. With your dog. What was his name, Buck?"

She gives me a withering look and I try again.

"Brick! I remember." My smile stretches thin. "Is he ok? He swallowed something, didn't he?"

This woman isn't up for making chit-chat this morning and I start to feel a little offended, but then I decide nobody's in a good mood when they haven't had their coffee yet and hurry to make her one. I'm watching Gabe and mimicking his movements and end up making something that looks sort of successful by the end of it, although I'm giving no guarantees for taste. Fortunately, Ms. Chatty-Pants has opted for a takeaway cup, so I slide a lid over my failed attempt at foam art and thrust the cup at her.

"Four dollars please."

She's eyeing the glass cabinet and taps one perfectly lacquered nail against it.

"And I'll take one of those cookies."

I fetch out one of the peanut ones and she squeals.

"Not one of those - the chocolate ones!"

"Sorry." I go to return it, but Jeremy is quicker at taking it off my hands. I exchange one pair of tongs for a clean one and carefully select the chocolate cookie furthest away from anything else, bag it up, and pass it to her, adding the price to her total.

"Thank you," she snaps, glaring at me, then Jeremy. Her cheeks flush and I realize she's noticed him for the first time, although I get the impression from Jeremy's awkward smile that he recognized her a lot sooner. "Jeremy." She sniffs, then tries to smile. "What are you doing here?"

"The same thing you are." He points to his cookie. "Coffee and snacks."

"Did you say coffee?" Gabe sails over and places a perfect macchiato in front of Jeremy, effectively breaking the spell.

"Right. Well, I'd better get going. I want to Facetime my boyfriend before my next showing." Ms. Uptight waves her smartwatch over the console and snatches up her coffee and her cookie, turning and stalking towards the door without a backward glance. I feel a chill wind gust around the coffee shop after her and somewhere in the back of my mind, the theme music for The Wizard of Oz's Wicked Witch of the West plays. I fix my gaze on Jeremy, who is studiously examining his peanut butter cookie but not actually eating it.

"You know her?"

"I knew her," he corrects, taking a dainty bite of his cookie. "We used to date."

I sigh. Well, that would explain her mood and the pointed mention of *my boyfriend* in front of Jeremy. It only takes the sight of my ex - husband, in my case, boyfriend in hers - to make even the brightest of days turn cloudy.

"Is there a single woman in this town whose heart you haven't broken?" I ask Jeremy sourly as I get back to work alongside Gabe, who's working like a machine, making more progress in minutes than I'm likely to manage all day.

"Yes." Jeremy blows me a kiss. "You!"

Chapter Three

Somewhere along the way, things slide into place and I even master the art of foam art - ish. Gabe is a more than capable assistant and during a rare lull, I ask him if he shouldn't be at school.

"Nope." He frowns. "I graduated last year."

"College, then." I tilt my head, curious that he seems perfectly content to stay put in Silver Brook. Almost every other teenager I know - which, to be fair, isn't many - can't wait to leave.

"I'm working for a while first," he said. "Got to save up." There's something practiced about his air of indifference and I back right off. I'm still struggling to balance my life and my checkbook after my divorce. I've bounced from short-term job to side hustle and never found anything that sticks. And judging from the amount of student loans I still have outstanding from my BA in *Nothing Anyone Wants to Hire Me For*, I don't have any good advice to offer anyone in the younger generation.

"It's just my mom and me," he says when I've been quiet a moment too long. "Business has been kind of slow for her lately, so I'm helping as much as I can."

Now it's my turn to break the awkward silence that's settled between us, and I do.

"I'm sure she's proud of your work ethic. Good for you! And even better for me! I'd never have managed today without you." I grimace. "I just know Maggie is going to come back to a disaster and regret ever asking for my help."

"You'll be fine," Gabe reassures me with a confidence I wish I could match. "Just remember the system." He performs a complicated set of dance moves in front of the coffee machine. "Left, right, left. Up, down, go!"

I'm still laughing when the bell over the door rings and I turn to greet our next customer, determined to complete this whole order by myself, just to prove I can do it.

"Morning, Merry!"

Officer Kate Kelly dashes into the cafe, waving as she passes me and makes a beeline for Jeremy. She stops just short of his table like she's only just realized it's him that's sitting there and offers him only a vague nod before turning on her heel and marching up to the counter. I guess she's taking my teasing about being the third wheel to their burgeoning new romance a little too seriously.

"Just a tea, please."

"Just a tea?" My smile falls. "And you were going to be my solo coffee practice run! Gabe's been teaching me all morning but it's time I step up to the plate and give it a shot." I pull a face. "Please?"

"Not today." Kate is all apologies. "Tea."

"I'll take a practice coffee," a smooth voice comes from somewhere behind my friend and we both turn our heads to see an impossibly handsome man waiting. My heart flips. An impossibly handsome *familiar* man.

"Dr. Castle!"

"Meredith Gray." His eyes twinkle as he looks at me. "You've saved me a journey." He reaches into the back pocket of his scrubs - what is it about a guy in scrubs, seriously? - and passes me a small box.

"For me?" My gaze drops and as I read what's written on the small box my nose wrinkles. *De-worming medication.* "For Snuffy." I smile, hoping he doesn't notice my awkwardness. "Thank you!"

"We forgot to give them to you this morning. Things got kind of hectic with that walk-in client after you."

"Right! The dog." My smile drops into a look of concern. "Is he alright?"

"He will be." Rob grimaces. "I'd be happier if I could get hold of his owner, though." He holds his phone up to me in frustration. "The number she gave doesn't exist and her address is for a house that's been empty for a month." He looks genuinely concerned and it takes me a minute to find my voice.

"You could ask Jeremy."

"What?"

"Jeremy - my friend - he knows her. Or knew her." I bustle out from behind the counter and drag Rob over to Jeremy's table. At some point during the last few minutes, Kate has drifted over to join him and they're sitting comfortably together.

"Merry!" Jeremy straightens, jerking his chair noisily and deliberately away from Kate. My friends are ridiculous. "What's up?"

"You remember that woman who came in here earlier? Ms. Chatty-Pants?"

"Ms. Davis," Rob puts in.

"Charlotte?" Jeremy darts a glance in Kate's direction but she's studying her fingernails and seems oblivious to all of us. "What about her?"

"I'm trying to get hold of her." Rob holds his phone up. "Vet business."

"She doesn't have any pets." Jeremy shakes his head. "Not a fan. Not a dog person. No cats."

Rob looks at me and I'm as bemused as he is.

"Well, dog person or not she's responsible for one at the moment. He's currently sleeping off an anesthetic in the back room of my clinic." He shrugs his shoulders. "And she was pretty keen to get her cufflinks back, so maybe that will motivate her more." He frowns and I can practically feel the annoyance radiating off him. I guess if anyone's going to disapprove of irresponsible pet owners it's a vet. "Do you have her number?"

Jeremy hesitates and for a long moment I think he's going to refuse. I wonder why he's being so prickly. *He's* not the one on the hook for the vet bill. *Or the dog.* I think sadly of Brick, then remind myself I've already rehomed one animal that fell on hard times and I certainly don't have room for another one. *Especially not a dog. Snuffy would not cope with that!* With one last look at Kate, and then at the table, Jeremy lets out a resigned sigh.

"Sure." He pulls out his phone, tapping away until he brings up Ms. Irresponsible Dog Owner's details, then angles his phone so Rob can take down her number. "You should try her sister, too. Emily." He thumbs through his contacts and I swear I see him blushing. It wouldn't surprise me if he's got a history with both of them. I eye Kate and silently pray she knows what she's getting herself into by dating him again.

"Her sister?" I can't resist asking. "Hold up. Emily Davis is that witch's sister?"

"That witch?" Rob glances my way, and I bite my lip, wishing I had a better hold on my tongue.

"They're twins," Kate pipes up. "But they aren't close. They don't exactly speak anymore. Ever since Charlotte stole Jason Reeves from her that summer a few years back."

I'd forgotten about that. It was the biggest scandal in Silver Brook, at least amongst my circle. Emily and Jack had been the golden couple until Charlotte moved back to town. Then, before you could even say *Benedict Arnold* Emily was single and there was a new golden couple in Silver Brook.

"They don't look alike," Kate continues, filling the silence. "Or act alike. You'd never know they were even sisters, let alone twins."

She can say that again. Emily Davis is one of the sweetest girls in town. If Brick belongs to her then I feel a lot happier about his prospects. Once he's back home where he belongs, with his actual owner instead of a disinterested dog-sitter, he'll be just fine.

"Emily Davis. Maybe I'll just call her directly, then. Thanks, you're a lifesaver." Rob smiles at me. "And thank *you*. If I'd known calling in here for a coffee would tick two out of three jobs off my to-do list I'd have done it sooner."

"Coffee!" I yelp, dashing back towards the counter.

"And I still want my tea, Merry!" Kate calls.

I fly into action, wishing that this was not the moment of all moments for Gabe to disappear. Kate's tea is easy, but I need all my concentration to make Rob's coffee. I hold my breath as the milk froths, determined to show off my newly acquired barista skills. I'm halfway through designing a simple leaf pattern when I decide to switch it up and get creative. Unfortunately, that instinct is one I definitely should have ignored. What I end up with isn't a leaf pattern or any kind of design at all. It's a splodgy, foaming mess. Swallowing my disappointment I lift it carefully in one hand, with Kate's tea in the other, and walk them over to my friends' table, noticing with dismay that Rob has pulled up a chair and is now chatting animatedly away. I pick up my pace, wincing when coffee sloshes over the side of the mug destroying whatever was left of my art attempt.

"Here we are!" I say brightly, dumping the drinks down on the table and surveying my friends with a nervous smile. "What are you guys talking about?"

"Our last date. Rob asked for suggestions of fun things to do in town." Jeremy grins but Kate at least has the sense not to meet my gaze.

"Oh?" My voice sounds weirdly high-pitched and I'm sure I can hear ringing in my ears. "And?"

"Well, we went to Rigg's shooting range," Kate says, trying to keep her voice casual, although I can see she's trying not to laugh. "My big-shot boyfriend thought he knew all there was to know about hitting a target from watching action movies."

"I never said that!" Jeremy protested.

"You certainly thought you'd be better at it than me, even though I have to use a gun for work."

"I didn't even know there was a shooting range near here," Rob puts in, smoothly averting a row. "Maybe I'll check it out sometime."

"Take Merry," Jeremy says. "She practically grew up there. Remember when Emily tried to get the place shut down and Mike Rigg kept sending you out to negotiate with her?" He chuckles and ignores the look I'm shooting at *him* right now. "And it worked, didn't it? The place is still here. Rob, you should see Merry in action. She's got better aim than all of us combined, so remember that before you think of upsetting her."

Jeremy. I wish he'd remembered my shooting skills before he thought of upsetting me. That thought softens the worst of my annoyance and I turn back towards the counter, praying for an escape from my friends. Gabe still isn't back, but I don't have any customers waiting, either. I've no reason not to stay right where I am. *And at least if I'm on hand, I can direct the rest of the conversation. Somewhat*. I pull out the fourth chair at their table and sit down, determined to take control of the situation.

"I took Snuffy for his jabs today," I say, praying my voice sounds more normal to my friends than it does to me. "He was very grumpy about it."

"But very well-behaved," Rob says, good-naturedly. "It was good to see him again. And it was good to see you again, Meredith." He's smiling at me and my stomach flutters. *Damn him*.

"Rob was just saying he's got a free night tonight."

Kate tries to silence Jeremy with a look but he's ignoring her, and I'm too far away to do much. I kick him under the table but miscalculate.

"Ow!"

"Oh no! I'm sorry!"

Rob bends down and rubs his shin. "I don't know if I'm up for firearms training. Maybe we could grab a bite to eat instead?" His words are sort of muffled and for a moment I don't hear him properly. He looks up at me. "What do you say? Or will you be too busy with this place?"

"Uh..."

"She'd love to!" Kate puts in, and I make a mental note to add her to my list along with Jeremy.

"How about *Pierre's*?"

"Eight o'clock?"

I could kill my friends. Both of them. Slowly. I can feel the blood flooding my cheeks and I try to breathe normally but before I can think of a proper response, Rob turns directly to me.

"Eight o'clock at *Pierre's*. Sounds good to me. See you there?" He picks up his coffee and takes a sip. "Hey, nice foam art. It's a hamster, right?" He winks. "How did you know that's my next patient?"

Chapter Four

By the time I finish work I'm exhausted, but the thought of an evening with gorgeous Rob gives me a little spring in my step...until I check my phone. There's a missed call and a message. *Still on for tonight? Pierre's is closed but I figured we could try Mrs. Wu's. Do you like Thai food?*

I tap out a quick reply and smile to myself, glad I got his message before I made it home. Pierre's is decidedly dressy and Mrs. Wu's is definitely...not.

"Goodbye little black dress," I mutter to myself as I fumble with my keys and open my door. "Hello, favorite jeans and a cute top." I'm certainly not going to complain about a more casual first date. I'm nervous enough without having to fret over candles and cutlery. I hit the lights as I enter the house and almost trip over Snuffy, who has planted himself right in the middle of the room for maximum impact when he pointedly ignores me. "And hello to you, Snuffy." I scoop him up for a hug which he only resists for a moment. He's purring before I even make it into the kitchen so I guess I'm forgiven for this morning's indignities. I give him a bigger dinner than usual and leave him happily chowing down while I dash upstairs to get ready.

After no less than three outfit changes, I dash out of the house again, desperate not to be late. I ought to be nervous, and probably if we were still going to Pierre's I would be. An evening at Mrs. Wu's feels less like a date-date, and the fact that I haven't had long to stew over it has helped keep the worst of my anxieties at bay. *The first time you met Rob somebody died. What's the worst that could happen tonight?* That thought opens the floodgates and I hurriedly shake my head to clear it. I don't need to remember that horrible Christmas when I stumbled - quite literally - over a dead body during my brief stint as Santa's Little Helper. *That was just bad luck*, I tell myself, repeating the comfort Kate has offered me more than once since then. *It's not like you seek out death and disaster.*

"I don't seek it out, but it seems to find me anyway..." I mutter grimly as I turn my car into the parking lot opposite Mrs. Wu's and glide into a space next to a suspiciously familiar-looking car. I angle my rear-view mirror, squinting into the reflection of the restaurant and soon see my recognition rewarded. "You have got to be kidding me!"

Climbing out of my car, I slam the door behind me and stalk across the road, narrowly avoiding being flattened by a truck driver who leans on his horn to remind me to watch where I'm going. I wave apologetically and keep moving, slipping into Mrs. Wu's and not bothering to look to see whether Rob's already arrived. My attention is fixed on another man, and I make a beeline for his table to give him a piece of my mind.

"Meredith?" Jeremy at least has the grace to look surprised to see me. "What are you doing here?"

"What am I doing here?" I seethe. "What are *you* doing here?"

"I..." He looks past me and starts shaking his head and I turn just in time to catch sight of Kate making her way towards the table with a drink in each hand. She freezes, then smiles at me, too wide.

"Merry! Aren't you going to be late for your date with Mr. Wonderful?"

"We rescheduled," I mutter, glancing from one of my so-called friends to the other. "Pierre's is closed. But I guess you knew that already. What, it wasn't enough for you to set me up on this date, you had to come and spy on me too?"

"What?"

"We're just keeping an eye on you," Kate says smoothly, as she shoves one glass into Jeremy's hand and slides past me into the empty chair opposite him. "That's all. But don't worry, we'll drink these and then head home." She takes a big gulp of her drink and then shoos me away. "Go on! You don't want to keep him waiting, do you?"

I don't, and I'm too stunned to think of anything else to say. In the end, I splutter something indecipherable and turn around to see Rob standing in the doorway, obviously waiting for me. I hurry over to join him, praying he hasn't noticed we have an audience. He's on his phone and as I get close I hear the tail end of his conversation. His voice is taut and agitated, completely different from the smooth baritone I'm used to hearing come out of his mouth.

"No, I don't think that's a justifiable reason. No - no, you don't understand. Wait - no, don't hang up, I -" He curses under his breath as whoever he was arguing with abruptly ends the call and I hesitate half a moment before leaning forward and tapping him lightly on the shoulder. He spins around so fast he drops his phone and it clatters noisily to the ground. "Merry! You startled me." He rakes a hand through his hair and stoops to retrieve his phone and for a moment I wonder if he'd rather cancel this evening. As he straightens, he's smiling again and I'm so star-struck I forget everything, even my own name. That is until another familiar voice reminds me of it.

"Good evening, Ms. Gray. Table for two?"

I turn and see Gabe lurking in the all-black uniform of a waiter. I frown, momentarily confused, which seems to delight him because he lets out a hoot of laughter.

"You look like you've seen a ghost. Come on, do you need a table or do you have one already booked?"

"What are you doing here?" I ask, too stunned by his presence to pay any notice to Rob's voice as he confirms our booking and we follow Gabe to a table in a quiet corner of the restaurant, far away from the prying eyes of my friends.

"Working." Gabe's grin stretches a little thin. "Mom's business has been a little slow so I'm picking up everything I can to help out."

"What does she do?"

"Real estate." Gabe brightens as he looks past me at Rob. "You in the market for a house?"

Before he can answer, I butt in with a question of my own.

"How many jobs do you have, Gabe?"

"Just these two." He shrugs. "Three, if you count holiday cover at Rigg's, not that he needs me at the moment. And soon, lawn mower season will kick in again..."

"Thanks very much," Rob takes the menu Gabe hands him and sits down, looking expectantly up at me until I follow his lead and drop into a chair opposite, wishing the ground would swallow me up. Not only my friends but also this kid who's technically my employee now get to witness me on the first date I've had since my marriage ended. Like I wasn't already nervous enough.

It's fine, I tell myself as Gabe takes a perfectly-timed break and I watch Rob pour himself and me a glass of water. *It's fine.*

Nothing else can go wrong tonight. Just relax. Enjoy yourself. You're on a date with Gorgeous Rob the Vet, and -

"I don't believe it."

Gorgeous Rob the Vet is scowling - actually *scowling* - as he looks at his phone and part of me wants to ask him if he's really happy to stay here when he clearly has business to sort out but then a movement over his shoulder catches my eye. Kate has been as good as her word. She's finished her drink and as she walks across the restaurant she catches my eye and waves, pulling a ridiculous kissy face at me that makes me duck down behind my menu and pray Rob doesn't notice my blush. At least one of my friends has taken me seriously. I turn my head and see Jeremy is still sitting right where I left him, lingering over his drink and tapping irritably on the table. That's not all. He's got company. Charlotte Davis sidles up to his table and he stands, all smiles, before leaning in for a hug.

Now it's my turn to scowl, and Rob is quick to notice it. He shoves his phone away and shoots me an apologetic smile.

"Sorry. I shouldn't be on my phone when I'm here with you...what's wrong?" He seems to realize the person I'm mad at isn't him and follows my gaze. "Oh, look who it is. Everybody's favorite dog-sitter."

"I'm more concerned about the guy she's on a date with," I spit out through gritted teeth. "Who has a *girlfriend*."

"Maybe it's not a date." Rob doesn't seem half as concerned as I am. "Maybe they're just catching up as friends. Everybody likes Thai food, right? And this place -"

He doesn't get long to finish his sentence. Jeremy downs the last of his drink and follows Charlotte out of the restaurant, too busy smiling and joking with her to notice the death glare I'm shooting his way.

"How do you feel about eating on the run?" I ask, jumping to my feet. "Because there's no way I'm letting my friend get her heart broken without doing something to stop it."

Rob argues - at least I think he does. I'm already walking out of the restaurant, my attention firmly fixed on Jeremy and Charlotte, who walk together to *his car* and climb inside. My heart is racing and I'm already imagining how much it's going to hurt to tell Kate that our friend Jeremy is not only up to his old tricks again, but he's somehow worse than ever. *Cheating on your current girlfriend with your ex-girlfriend? And five minutes after she's gone home? That is lower than low, Jeremy. I can't believe you!*

"You could just call him, you know," Rob points out, as he jogs to keep pace with me.

"And let him lie to me?" I shake my head. "No. I need to see what's going on for myself. Then I can decide what to tell Kate." I look at him, my eyes bright with anger and adventure. "Where did you park your car?" I can't use mine. It's parked right next to Jeremy and would alert him to the fact that I'm onto him. Rob seems to pick up what I'm putting down. He sighs, then points in the opposite direction to where my so-called friend is fiddling with his music choice for their journey to hell. "Excellent. We're going on an intelligence-gathering mission. You can drive."

"Alright." He doesn't sound entirely convinced, and for a moment I think I've pushed things too far and ruined our first date before it's even begun. Then he smiles. "But after that, we're coming back here and getting a takeaway, deal?"

"Deal."

Chapter Five

"Turn left here," I whisper, as I see Jeremy take a turn off the long, straight road we've been following him along. "No wait, let him get a little further ahead of us."

"Why are you whispering?" Rob asks, speaking at a perfectly normal volume.

"I...don't know." I bite my thumbnail, my heart still jackhammering in my chest. Rob reaches across and turns the radio on and there's a screech of guitars that makes me jump.

"Sorry." Rob smiles and hits a few buttons until something smooth and jazzy flows out of the speakers. He eyes me and turns the volume down until it's barely noticeable. "Where now?" We've made the turn as I instructed but somewhere in the distance, Jeremy has disappeared. I lean forward, squinting into the darkness and that's when I realize he hasn't disappeared - he's parked up.

"Stop the car!"

Rob obediently slams on the breaks and we come to a sudden, noisy stop.

"Sorry." There's a note of something that might be annoyance in his voice, and he slides the car over to park on the side of the road. I glance at him, wishing I could read his expression but it's particularly blank just now. Still handsome, though. His eyes meet mine and I offer him a sheepish, apologetic smile.

"I guess this wasn't the evening you planned on."

"Not exactly." He turns off the engine and follows my gaze to where Jeremy is following Charlotte Davis up the darkened street to a shadowy house. "You really think he's cheating on your friend?"

"It certainly looks that way." I sigh and go back to chewing on my thumbnail, a habit I've just about given up trying to quit. "Kate's going to be heartbroken."

"Maybe it isn't what it looks like," Rob offers, hopefully. I shoot him a look and his smile drops. "So what do you want to do? If you want to spend all night staking the place out, I'm happy to, but we are going to need some snacks." His eyes sweep over me. "I don't suppose you have any leftover pastries from the Jitterbug on you, do you?"

I dip into my purse and pull out half a roll of mints and with a laugh, he slides two into his mouth.

"Thank you. This will keep me going."

"We won't be here all night," I promise. "I just need to figure out what to do next." I pull out my phone, my thumb hovering over Kate's number when I hear a door slam. I look back at the house and see Jeremy making his way out of the shadows, a grin on his obnoxious, jerky face.

"Are you going to talk to him?" Rob asks. I figure he can tell I'm frozen in indecision, and in one moment I make a choice.

"Nope." I wait until Jeremy is out of sight, then I fling open my car door. "I'm going to talk to her!"

"Wait! Merry -"

He follows me, but I'm quicker, and I have the rage of a thousand wronged women powering my steps as I march towards the dim house. There's only one light on that I can see, but if Jeremy came out alone that means Charlotte is still in here. *And it's about time I gave her a piece of my mind. For Kate, for Emily, and for me!* Ok, she didn't actually steal any guy from me, but she's crossed me twice today and I'm just itching to tell her off. *What about the sisterhood? What about your actual, literal sister!?* I remember how heartbroken Emily was that summer when she lost Jason to her own sister. Their fling didn't last long and Jason was so ashamed of himself that he promptly left Silver Brook, leaving Emily to rebuild her life alone. *And I know exactly how hard that is.* My divorce is still casting a shadow over my present happiness.

I jab my finger into the doorbell and when that doesn't bring an immediate response I knock. Then again. I'm about to knock a third time when Rob tries the handle and to his surprise as much as mine, it yields easily and the door swings open.

There's a weird, sinister silence in the darkened house, and for a moment I falter, all the words I had stored up to say disappearing with what's left of my confidence. Rob is still standing next to me, and he seems to sense that I need his support.

"Hello?" His voice is enough to urge me forward and I step over the threshold, listening for any kind of response. There's a sound I recognize, the crack of a gun, then another, and I move towards it until Rob's hand closes on my shoulder, pulling me back behind him. "Wait."

"Did you hear that?" I ask, shrugging him off. "Charlotte? Are you here?"

Rob moves ahead of me and I sense his concern which only makes my heart race even faster. I follow him towards the noise and we burst into an empty kitchen, lit only by the light over the stove. The back door bangs on its hinges and Rob moves towards the door, oblivious to the sight that has me pinned in place, my mouth open in a stunned, silent scream.

Charlotte is lying on the floor, a look of shock frozen on her face, as two gunshots pool blood from her stomach.

• • • •

"I CAN'T BELIEVE THIS has happened again."

I'm sitting on the floor in the empty living room, the other side of the wall from the kitchen where we found Charlotte's body.

Charlotte's body. Another dead body. I'm beginning to wonder if I'm cursed. Rob is sitting next to me and he slides his arm around me. I silently lean into him, grateful that he's here. He sprang into action, dropping to his knees next to Charlotte and performing what little first aid he could. That was when we realized she wasn't dead - at least not yet. She tried to say something but before I could understand what, Rob threw his phone at me and told me to call an ambulance, which I did, and the police, which I did right after, my hands shaking as I tapped in the numbers. The ambulance came quickly and relieved Rob, and it was then he turned his attention to me, checking I was ok after what we'd stumbled into. *This isn't my first rodeo*, I felt like saying, then wondered what possessed me to make jokes at a time like this. In the end, I didn't say anything at all, just stood back and allowed the paramedics to work. It wasn't until the police chief arrived that he told us both to go and wait in the next room.

"Who lives here, do you think?" I asked, looking around the empty living room. When we'd walked through here I hadn't noticed there wasn't any furniture but now, even with only the low light from the doorway illuminating the room I can see just how cavernously empty it is.

"It's for sale," Rob says, brushing at the blood stains on his jeans. "Charlotte was a realtor."

"Oh."

I shake my head, not wanting to think about it. Poor Charlotte. Whatever else she was, she didn't deserve this.

"Will she be ok, do you think?"

Rob takes a minute to answer, and even though he nods and smiles neither action is very convincing.

"They'll take good care of her," he promises, which is I guess the only reassurance he can offer me.

The door to the kitchen opens and we both scramble to our feet as Police Chief Trainor steps into the room, squints at us, then hits a switch that bathes the room in bright, electric light.

"Meredith Gray." He looks at me. "And Rob Castle. Mind if have a word?"

"Sure." I glance at Rob, who nods, but before I can open my mouth the police chief holds up a hand to stop me.

"Actually, Ms. Gray I'll speak to Dr. Castle first, if that's ok. Do you mind waiting...ah..." He glances around and for one horrifying moment I think he's going to send me back into the kitchen which is swarming with crime scene investigators.

"Why doesn't Merry wait here," Rob says, suggesting he and the police chief go back into the other room. I'm grateful, even though their leaving means I'm completely alone in the room now, which I also hate. I'm almost tempted to follow them when the door opens and to my surprise, Kate walks in. She's pale and her features look sort of pinched and unnatural but I'm still pleased to see her.

"Hi, Merry," she says, her voice thin. "Chief Trainor said I might as well come and take your statement." She looks around for somewhere to sit, but in the end, we both end up cross-legged on the floor. She lays her phone down between us, opens up a voice recording app, and asks me to describe what happened.

"Rob and I knocked on the door but it wasn't locked, and we let ourselves in. We were looking for Charlotte, to -" I look at Kate and hesitate, wondering how to explain just why I'd been looking for Charlotte. "We were looking for Charlotte," I continue, hoping that question just won't come up. "And there was a noise in the kitchen. We followed it and that's when we - when we found her. She was lying on the ground and she'd been hurt. Rob tried to help her and I called an ambulance, and the police, and...that's it." I swallow past a lump in my throat. "Have you heard anything from the hospital? Is she going to be ok?"

"I don't know," Kate says, quietly. She's tugging at a thread on her cuff and we end up sitting in near silence for a long minute until Kate leans over and switches off her recording. "Have you seen Jeremy anywhere tonight?"

"Do you mean after running into both of you at the restaurant?" I can hear the sharp, false note in my voice and I'm sure Kate can see right through me. I've never been any good at lying, especially to my friends.

"Officer Kelly! Here you are!" Chief Trainor bustles back into the room and looks directly at me. "Good, you've taken Ms. Gray's first statement? Excellent. Well, it's still early but I think we have our first person of interest. Do either of you know..." He glances at his notepad and my heart sinks. I know exactly whose name he's going to share before he says it, but it still stings. "Jeremy Walton?" I risk a glance at Kate and she looks as anxious as I feel.

"Yes sir, I know him," she says, wearily. "He's my boyfriend."

Chapter Six

I f there's one place to be the morning after a sleepless night, it's a coffee shop. I've had plenty of chances to perfect my methods by making drinks just for me, and it's a good job I'm feeling more confident in my barista abilities because there's been a steady stream of customers coming and going all morning. Half of Silver Brook has been into the Jitterbug Junction for their morning brew - and to gossip about the latest disaster to strike our small town.

"It's awful of course," Pat Cooper remarks as I make her a latte with three shots of caramel syrup. She's counting out sugar packets to go with it and my pancreas clenches in sympathy but I just nod and hand her the drink. "And I'd never say she asked for it, but..."

"Oh?" I try to keep my tone light but this is about the third customer I've had this morning who's suggested that Charlotte Davis got what was coming to her.

"Well, she wasn't very well-liked, was she, dear?" Pat hands over her money, then takes her coffee and her sugars and drifts over to join a little clutch of neighbors all busily discussing who might be behind this crime and whether it's likely to be repeated.

"Anyone would think Silver Brook isn't a safe place to live!" Gabe remarks, next to me. He's still a great help and seems much more adept at fending off the questions and comments of our more grisly customers. "Although I guess that depends on how you choose to live your life."

"Oh, not you too!" I frown at him. "Whatever Charlotte Davis did or didn't do doesn't give anyone the right to -"

"Quiet!" Gabe has quicker reactions than me: he's spotted the latest arrival at the Jitterbug and turns to greet her with a sympathetic smile. "Good morning, Emily! How are you?"

"Well, hello to you too, Gabe! I'm doing just fine thank you!" Emily Davis catches my eye and waves. "Morning, Merry!"

"Morning." I can't stop staring at Charlotte's sister. The pair never looked particularly alike, despite being twins, but this morning there's something about Emily's face that is more than a little reminiscent of her missing sister. She's wearing much more makeup than she usually would, and there's a sparkle in her eyes that makes her seem almost...happy. My heart lifts. "Have you had news from the hospital?"

Emily's head tilts to one side. She can't hear me over the roar of the milk frother and I wait until Gabe's finished before asking my question again.

"Did the hospital call with an update on your sister? How is she doing?"

"Your guess is as good as mine." Emily shrugs her shoulders. "I haven't heard, and I don't know that I'd be first on their list to call. We weren't exactly close, Merry, you know that." Her smile tightens. "Of course, it's dreadful what happened to her, but..."

There it was again. That "but". As if Charlotte was the kind of person who everyone knew might get hurt one day, and who just might deserve it. I frown. *Does everybody in Silver Brook feel like this?*

I'm kind of struck dumb for a moment until Emily points at the pastry case between us. "Are those blueberry scones? They look lovely!"

"Here." I plate one up and pass it to her stiffly. "On the house."

"Well, aren't you the sweetest!" She smiles. "Thank you!"

A wave of silence ripples through the cafe as Emily makes her way to a table in the window and I see a dozen curious faces turn her way. I can't take my eyes off her myself, and fight a shiver of unease at just how ok Charlotte's sister seems to be in the wake of her sister's attack.

"You see?" Gabe mutters as he cleans the countertop in front of me. "Not even her sister is heartbroken that she's gone."

"In the hospital," I correct. "She's going to be fine."

I sense Gabe's look of disbelief and try to ignore it, repeating my words to myself almost like saying them a second time will make them true. "She's going to be just fine."

Fortunately, neither of us has long to dwell on things. Business is booming today and I just have time to slide another tray of pastries into the oven to warm through before I dash back through to cover the counter so Gabe can finally take a break. I'm juggling orders when Kate comes in, looking even worse than she did last night.

"Sit here!" I insist, pointing to one of the stools nearest me. "I'll make you a drink." I hurry through the orders for my next three customers and practically push them back through the door so I can give all my attention to my friend. I throw together her usual order, then plate up the last two of my pick-me-up peanut butter cookies and hand them to her. "What's wrong?"

"Everything." Kate picks morosely at the corner of one cookie and when she looks at me I can see dark circles under her eyes. I know I don't look so crash-hot today but she looks even worse. "Chief Trainor put me on canvassing." She rolls her eyes and takes a noisy slurp of her coffee. "I'm supposed to spend all day walking around Silver Brook talking to people."

"About what happened?" I drop my voice, certain my other customers would all be listening in if they could. Kate shakes her head.

"About everything but that." She draws in a shaky breath. "He's taken me off the case. Says I'm too close to it. I might compromise the investigation."

"Why?" I'm racking my brains trying to think in what world my sensible friend Kate would have had anything to do with either Charlotte Davis or the person who attacked her when Kate spells out the reason.

"Chief Trainor thinks Jeremy had something to do with it. And as he's my boyfriend, I can't be seen to have any involvement with the investigation."

"Jeremy?!" My voice is a little louder than I mean it to be and I see several heads lift and turn my way, their curious eyes wide at the notion of gossip. I survey the crowd but can't count Emily's face among them. She must have finished up her coffee and slipped out sometime when I wasn't looking. That's one thing to be grateful for. The last thing I want is for Charlotte Davis's sister to catch me gossiping about her sister's attack. Even if she didn't seem unduly upset about it, she doesn't need to know my opinion. I force a smile and a wave and turn back to my friend, this time keeping my voice below a whisper. "They think Jeremy had something to do with it? But he can't! I saw him leave -" I stop talking all at once, but Kate's looking at me like she knows I know a whole lot more than I'm admitting to. I swallow past a lump in my throat and then decide to tell her everything. "Look, Jeremy is the reason I was there. Me and Rob, I mean. We saw him - that is, I saw him - he left Mrs. Wu's with - with that woman and I got so mad when I thought of him cheating on you that I…told Rob to follow them."

"You did what?"

"We followed them. But that's what I mean. Jeremy left the house before we went in. Before Charlotte…I mean, he couldn't…he wouldn't…" I glance at my watch and begin hastily pouring out coffee into takeaway cups. "Gabe will be back off his break any minute now. And when he is, I'm going to run over to the police station with some coffees and pastries and see if I can't find out what's going on." I offer Kate what I hope is an encouraging smile. "And I'm going to make sure Chief Trainor knows that Jeremy wasn't anywhere near Charlotte when she was attacked. He might be a cheat, but he certainly isn't a killer."

"He's not a cheat," Kate mumbles into her coffee and I haven't the heart to contradict her. What good is going to do to upset her now? Better get Jeremy out of this mess and let him fight his own way out of that one. *And he can manage Kate without my help. As long as he manages to stay out of trouble long enough to do it.*

Chapter Seven

The lobby of the police station is surprisingly quiet when I push open the door and make my way inside. I take a deep breath, adjust my stance a little, and shoot for *casual* rather than *curious*, hoping I don't look as nervous as I feel. It isn't my first time inside the Silver Brook police station. When you live so long in a small town you end up seeing the inside of practically everywhere, and there's been more than one occasion I've stopped by to visit Kate when she's been working late catching up on paperwork and such, but being here in the middle of an active investigation is a whole different feeling. Especially when it's an investigation I have a vested interest in.

"Hello?" I make my way to the reception desk, surprised to find that, too, is deserted. Everybody knows Marjorie Becker, the station receptionist, is practically glued to the front desk and her phone when she's working here. She knows everybody - and everybody's business - and if I'd hoped she might be my key to finding out what's going on with Jeremy, it looks like I'm going to be disappointed. Well, I've never been one to fall at the first hurdle. I raise my voice, injecting just the right note of cheer into it. "Hello! Chief Trainor? I brought snacks...!"

There's no reply but I can hear muffled voices and that's the direction I head for, scooting around Marjorie's empty desk and along a corridor lined with closed, locked doors. At least, mostly closed. The third on the right is open like a half an inch and I freeze, holding my breath to hear what's going on on the other side.

"So you don't deny you were there last night?"

"No." That's Jeremy's voice. He sounds exhausted, like he's trying to stay patient even though I get the feeling he's given this answer a dozen times already. "I already told you. I had a meeting with Charlotte at the house and when I left she was just fine."

"A meeting?" I can practically hear Chief Trainor's air quotes around the word "meeting" and I wonder if he's going to get Jeremy to admit it was a date. I'm not sure what answer I want to hear, but in the end I get none, because Marjorie chooses that moment to burst out of a store cupboard, weighed down with office supplies. She spots me and lets out a yelp of surprise before dropping two reams of paper and a box of loose stationery noisily to the ground, sending pens, push-pins, and a hundred other things skittering in all directions.

"Meredith!" she claps a hand against her chest. "You scared me!"

"What's going on out there?" That's Chief Trainor's voice and I don't have time to move before the door opens and he's standing there, blocking my view of the small room - and of Jeremy - with a frown on his face I just know he perfected to scare Silver Brook's reprobates into confessing on the spot. It kind of works, until I remember my pre-packed reason for being there.

"I brought you guys some snacks!" I say, brightly. "And coffees! I left them on Marjorie's desk. She wasn't there, so I…"

"I was doing a stationery audit," Marjorie wails. She's kneeling on the floor and is furiously trying to gather up her loose supplies and I bend down to help her, wanting to make myself useful and hoping that Chief Trainor will be too distracted to think about what I was really up to.

"You brought coffee?" he asks. I crane my neck to look up at him and he's even more terrifying from this angle. I thrust my arm up, passing him the bag of treats.

"And freshly baked doughnuts."

He's wavering. I see him almost reach for the bag, then yank his hand back.

"Well, that's mighty kind of you, Ms. Gray. You can leave them with Marjorie." He clears his throat. "Once you...ah...finish clearing this up."

He disappears back into the room and closes the door firmly behind him and I sigh. I won't be able to glean anything else from there this morning.

"Here." I shove a handful of pens onto Marjorie's messily-reconstructed pile of office supplies and we both get wearily to our feet. "Sorry I scared you."

"That's alright, dear," Marjorie says, eyeing my paper bag. "Did you really bring us doughnuts?"

"And coffee," I say, glancing back over my shoulder in one last vain attempt to discover something that I can take back to Kate at the cafe.

"Why don't you stay and have one with me?" she asks, bustling us both back towards the main desk. "I think the police chief is going to be in there a while, and everyone else seems to be busy today what with the -" She drops her voice. "Murder."

"Murder? I thought Charlotte was recovering in the hospital." My heart sinks and my features must match it because once Marjorie drops her armfuls of supplies on her desk she turns to me with a sad shake of her head.

"Didn't you hear? That poor girl passed away. So now Chief Trainor is trying to solve a murder." She draws in a wary breath.

"And nobody's going to get even a minute's peace until they figure it out." She shivers. "I mean, who can relax when someone is running around the town with a gun?" She shakes her head with a stern scowl. "I place the blame on that Mr. Rigg and his shooting range. And then there's all the violent movies and video games these days."

I'm still standing numbly clinging onto my paper bag of treats and she seems to realize, too late, that I have more interest than most of Silver Brook in catching whoever is responsible for Charlotte Davis's death. Her demeanor changes in an instant, from judgy and irritable to sympathetic.

"Oh, you poor dear! You found the - the -" She pauses. "You found *her*, didn't you?" She takes me by the arm and steers me into a chair, then loosens my grip on the doughnuts, sliding them out of my hands and dumping them on her desk next to the coffee cups that sit, untouched and slowly going cold. "Sit down. We'll have a nice cup of coffee and something to eat."

There's something so wonderfully motherly about Marjorie that I don't say no. It's actually kind of nice having someone take care of me for a change, and we decide to only split one of the doughnuts, so there's plenty left for the rest of the officers, even though I doubt the coffees will be any good to them cold.

Marjorie is chattering away to me about her grandson's latest success in school - skilfully trying to distract me from more morbid topics of conversation - when the phone rings and she swiftly lifts the receiver, her voice clipped and businesslike.

"Silver Brook Police Station, Marjorie speaking. How may I help you?"

The person on the other end of the line is agitated, even I can hear that, though I can't tell what they're saying.

"No, no. That's just fine. Calm down, Mr. Montgomery. Tell me again. Yes...yes...Lattimer Street."

I freeze, my coffee cup halfway to my lips, and watch Marjorie carefully. Lattimer street? That's where Charlotte lives! My stomach churns. *Lived.*

"A disturbance you say? Well no, you don't need to go and investigate. I'll send the police over right away. Thank you for calling. Thank you! Goodbye!"

She jumps to her feet and is halfway down the corridor before she remembers me.

"Stay there, Meredith! I'll be right back!"

I am not going anywhere. Something's happening - something connected to the case, and something they can't hold against Jeremy if he's trapped here while somebody else is out there disturbing Charlotte Davis's empty house. I sip my coffee and strain to hear what Marjorie's excited, high-pitched voice is saying to Chief Trainor, who bursts noisily out of the room and into the lobby. He's jamming his hat on his round, balding head and doesn't seem to notice me as he barks orders at Marjorie, who darts around him like an excitable spaniel.

"Call Officer Kelly - no, I told her...better make it Stephens. Tell him to meet me at the address. I'll go straight there." He barrels out of the door leaving me and Marjorie staring after him.

"I wasn't able to ask him about..." She frowns, eyeing the rapidly cooling cups of coffee. "I wonder if..." She looks at me, and I do my best to look innocent, hoping that might help her to finish a thought. "Stay here." She says, lifting one of the untouched coffee cups and bustling off down the corridor and into the room where I know they're holding Jeremy. *Well,* I think, taking a sip of my coffee. *At least I know he's getting something decent to drink.*

The front door of the police station swings open and I flinch, half expecting to see Chief Trainor coming back with another machine-gun list of instructions for Marjorie, but it isn't the police chief. It's Rob, and his green eyes widen as they fix on me.

"Merry! What are you doing here?"

"Drinking coffee," I say stupidly. "I mean…delivering coffee. And snacks." I point at the bashed, deflated paper bag and wonder if anyone will ever actually eat the doughnuts I brought.

"Right."

He straightens and I see there's something clutched in his hands. He notices me notice and folds them behind him with a brief smile.

"I'm looking for Chief Trainor. Is he around?"

"He just left." I take a noisy sip from my coffee cup and keep looking at Rob, wondering when things changed between us. *When he incriminated my friend in a murder.* "Did you want to make a change to your statement?" I ask, hoping Rob will say yes. Instead, he frowns and then shows me what he is hiding. A small ziploc bag containing two sparkling diamond cufflinks.

"I thought he ought to have these. They're evidence."

"From the crime scene?" *And what are they doing in your possession?*

"Ah, no." He shifts his weight awkwardly from one foot to another. "From Brick."

"Who?"

I choke on my coffee as I remember who Brick is and just where this evidence might have come from.

"Yeah..." Rob winces. "Anyway, when I mentioned Charlotte Davis bringing the dog in to see me yesterday, Chief Trainor was interested. She said they belonged to some boyfriend nobody had even heard of. I said I'd bring these along and see if they belonged to...Jer - to his suspect."

"Jeremy isn't a suspect!" I protest when I finally get my breath back. "You know he'd left the house by the time we got there."

"I know he was there to begin with. Even you thought that was suspicious."

"Yeah, because I thought he was cheating on my friend, not because -" I hear Marjorie's kitten heels tap-tapping on the floor and lower my voice. "I can't believe you think he's capable of murder."

"People are capable of all sorts of things, Merry, even when they're our friends, and -"

I stand, suddenly too hurt to sit here a moment longer. I don't want to be faced with the fact that Rob Castle isn't who I thought he was, and that he might be responsible for my friend getting blamed for something he didn't do.

"I have to go."

I stride past him, not even waiting to say goodbye to Marjorie, and head back to the Jitterbug, sad to see my fleeting hopes of romance dashed before they even start. *It's probably for the best*, I tell myself, trying to get a hold of my feelings before I have to see people again. *Romance is overrated. You either end up like Emily - and me, after my marriage breakdown - heartbroken. Or Charlotte*. I shudder. *Dead.*

Chapter Eight

When I get back to the cafe the first person to catch my eye is Kate, and when I shake my head she looks so upset I almost want to go back and try again. I'm hatching an elaborate plan to jailbreak Jeremy out of the police station when the sound of a muted argument breaks through my reverie.

"Gabe?" I spot my employee's head bent close to an older woman, who has her hand clamped like a vice around his arm. "Is everything ok?"

"Oh, sure." He yanks his arm free and turns to me with his usual grin. "We're fine. This is my mom."

"Mrs. Matthews! Hi!" Now that he's introduced me I can see a resemblance and I figure their body language makes a lot more sense. I'm sure if I had a teenage boy to wrangle I'd get a little irritable at times too. "Can I get you anything?" I start to clear up behind the counter and do a quick check on our pastries and coffee situation, making a mental note of what needs refilling first.

"I'm fine, thank you. Just stopped to talk to Gabe about something."

She sounds kind of cagey and when I glance back at her I see she's staring into her son's eyes like their argument isn't over. I turn away to give them some privacy and lean over to talk to Kate.

"No joy at the police station," I say. "Jeremy was still in there when I left, but Chief Trainor got called away, so hopefully that's a good sign."

"Hmm." Kate doesn't seem convinced. I wonder if I should be more worried than I am. If they only had Rob's testimony to go on that should be easy enough to disprove. I was quick to explain that *I* saw Jeremy leave, and surely that's enough to at least cast a bit of doubt on Rob's report. But those cufflinks.

"Hey, does Jeremy own a pair of diamond cufflinks?"

"What?" Kate frowns at my question. "I don't know. Maybe? It's not like I have his whole wardrobe memorized."

"Right." I still don't think it's the end of the world. Just because Charlotte was cagey about her dog having swallowed those particular cufflinks doesn't mean they were in any way linked to her death, right? *And Brick wasn't even her dog*, I remind myself. My gaze strays to the corner booth where Emily had been sitting earlier and I wonder if she's been reunited with her furry friend yet.

"I can't believe they're not letting me help figure this out," Kate grumbles, scrolling listlessly on their phone. "I did pretty well at solving the last murder that happened in Silver Brook."

"In that case, maybe the police station should look at hiring me," I say, trying to lighten the mood and failing. I'm still job-hopping at the moment, and running the Jitterbug is all well and good until Maggie comes back, but she won't be away for long and I'm going to need something stable sooner rather than later. "I wonder if there's much call for detectives in the wild."

Kate eyes me and I can see she's unsure whether to laugh at me or take me seriously.

"I mean, there's plenty of reasons people might hire a private investigator, isn't there? Background checks, business deals, questionable relationships..." I remember how convinced I was that Jeremy was cheating on Kate last night and drop my gaze.

It's the last thing I want to bring up now, but she's so distracted she doesn't seem to notice.

"You'd have to be good at computers," she says, tapping at her phone. "Everything's online these days."

"Not everything." I'm defensive. "And I do just fine with the socials." I wince. That's possibly the first time I've ever used the phrase *the socials* and it sticks out like a sore thumb. "And you know I've always loved a good murder mystery book. My aunt Cassie got me hooked on them when I was a kid, and now we trade our favorites."

"That's nice." Kate isn't listening to me, and I give up trying to cheer her up. Gabe's mom seems to have calmed down and he's sitting with her at a table in the corner, holding her hand and speaking in a low, comforting tone. I worry that this is another personal disaster unfolding right here in front of us and something in me wants to wade in and help if I can. Mrs. Matthews has that same exhausted, haunted look that I've seen on enough people when the bottom falls out of their world. I got used to seeing it each time I looked in the mirror for a while until I finally started to rebuild my life without Neil there to derail everything. *And I did a pretty good job*, I tell myself. *Even if I don't have the thriving career part settled quite yet.*

The door to the cafe swings open and I look up, expecting the start of another rush of customers. It's only one person - but someone I'm so pleased to see I can't help but smile. I clear my throat and Kate looks up, then follows my gaze to see who I've just spotted.

"Jeremy!" She jumps out of her chair and runs to throw her arms around him and I realize, whatever else is going on between them, at this moment they are happy. I'm happy too, that my best friend doesn't seem to be still stuck in the police station, being blamed for a crime he didn't commit.

"What happened?" I ask, making him a coffee without even asking what he wants. I grab a handful of the peanut butter cookies I know he loves and set it all down in front of me, urging him and Kate to come back and sit down. "Did they let you go?"

"For now." Jeremy offers me a tired smile and reaches for a cookie. "They aren't finished with me yet but there isn't anything they can use to keep me there. Chief Trainor told me not to leave town." He rolled his eyes. "Where am I going to go?"

"That's just standard," Kate reassures him. She's hanging off his arm like she's worried about letting go of him. "We'll get this all cleared up soon, I promise."

"Right." Jeremy meets my gaze and I see a shadow flicker across his face.

"You shouldn't have been there at all!" I say as I hand him a drink. "I told the police you'd already left by the time we..."

He's still staring at me and I realize he doesn't know that I was one of the people who put him at the crime scene to begin with.

"By the time you what, Meredith?" He's gripping his coffee cup so tightly that his knuckles are white.

"You know Merry and Rob were there," Kate says, in a low voice. "They found Charlotte when...when she was hurt."

"Yeah, what were you guys doing there, anyway?" Jeremy asks, undeterred by Kate's soothing voice. "I thought you were having your date at Mrs. Wu's."

"We were..." I glance over to Gabe and his mom and see they're arguing again, their voices gradually rising. She leans across the table to take hold of Gabe's hand but he shrugs her off, standing and stalking past her towards the door.

"Gabe!"

"I'm taking a break," he yells over his shoulder, but as he passes his mom's chair, his foot catches her bag by the handle and knocks it over, tipping all of its contents all over the floor. Everyone turns to look, and a few people bend down to help until Kate spots something nobody else has yet.

"Wait!" She's in police-procedure mode at once, striding forward to retrieve the item that has her attention. She picks it up carefully, avoiding getting any of her fingerprints on it as much as she can. My blood freezes in my veins and I see the color drain from Mrs. Matthews's - and Gabe's - faces as we all look at what Kate's holding. A gun.

Chapter Nine

"**I**t's not what it looks like!"

Mrs. Matthews is the first to speak. She makes a grab for the gun but Kate's reflexes are quicker and she takes a hurried step back, glancing over her shoulder at Jeremy and me.

"I should take this into the station."

"Why?" Mrs. Matthews smiles and tries to make light of the whole thing. "It's my gun. I have the papers for it." She reaches into her bag, pulls out a wedge of paperwork she starts shuffling through until she finds the pieces she's looking for. She holds it out for Kate to look at. "Well, I can't find the papers right now but I promise you It's mine, and I have a license for it and everything."

"Why do you need to carry a gun?" I ask, unable to keep my mouth shut any longer. My eyes trail around the rest of my customers and I wonder how many others are smuggling weapons in perfectly normal-looking clutch purses.

"For protection." Mrs. Matthews' smile dims. "And judging from what happened to poor Charlotte, it looks like I need it." She holds her hand out flat, palm up. "Please can I have it back now, Kate? If you need me to come to the police station and make a statement I can do that." She glances at her son, then looks back in Kate's direction. I sense a trace of defiance in her gaze. "I do have an alibi for last night, if that's what you're concerned about."

Kate frowns, but she's clearly reluctant to give the weapon back. In the end, she has to. There's no reason for her to keep it when Mrs. Matthews has every legal right to have it with her.

"Do you know how to shoot it?" Kate asks, brushing her hands against each other and watching as the older woman stows the gun away out of sight. "Safely, I mean."

"Well, certainly. Yes. I've been to Rigg's shooting range. I wanted to learn how to use it and how to look after it. For safety. I don't want any accidents."

A cool silence blows through the cafe. What happened to Charlotte wasn't an accident, and I'm pretty sure that's what Kate is thinking. But she can't suspect Gabe's mom, surely? There's no reason the person who shot her would be so open about having a gun in the first place, let alone bragging about how well she knows how to use it.

"Well, alright," Kate says, with a long sigh. "But I'll have to make a note of it. We're waiting for a list of Rigg's customers anyway, so I'll be able to see that you're on it."

"Good." Mrs. Matthews lets out a high-pitched laugh of relief and turns back to her son. "Well, I'd better get back out there. I have appointments all afternoon and a couple out in Monroe Cove. Will you be home for dinner?"

Gabe nods, very subdued, and I wonder just what he and his mom were arguing about before this. He looks past her to me and I smile, hoping I seem encouraging.

"Go on and take a break, Gabe. I didn't mean to leave you here running the place alone for so long."

He nods again and continues his way out of the cafe and it seems like every single one of us watches him leave.

"I'd better get a move on too," Mrs. Matthews says. She hurries up to the counter to pay for the drink she barely touched and I wave her off.

"No charge! Perks of having such a great son," I say, with a wide smile. *And an apology for thinking you were a murderer for a minute there.* I hope she can't see the blush I feel heating my cheeks. She doesn't seem to, just wishes me a good rest of the day, and dashes out of the cafe, her phone pressed to her ear as she makes plans for the afternoon.

"Nice lady," Jeremy remarks, around a mouthful of peanut butter cookie.

"Yeah, apart from her gun habit."

Jeremy side-eyes Kate, then looks at me. I can see the corners of his lips twitch and busy myself with clearing up so that I only hear a little bit of their good-natured bickering.

"I have to carry one for my work!" I can just about hear Kate's shrill protest as I duck back into the kitchen to whip up another batch of cookies. I feel a little more at ease now I know Jeremy isn't the prime suspect for Charlotte's death, but my good mood only lasts so long. Whoever is responsible for hurting her is still out there. And if we don't know who killed her or why, that means they might strike again, soon.

An image of Rob's face swims up before me and I remember how comfortable it felt to lean into his arms after the police arrived at the house. I wish things were still the same between us as they were then. It wasn't his fault that Jeremy had been caught up in all this. He just told them exactly what we'd seen - that Jeremy had met with Charlotte and gone with her to the house. He was very likely the last person to see her before she was attacked. I frown, wondering just what Jeremy was doing there after all.

"Merry! I have to go, ok? They're calling me back into work!"

I hurry back into the cafe just in time to wave goodbye to Kate and to my relief Jeremy is still sitting there, lingering over his coffee. I walk slowly towards him and as if he can feel my eyes on him he sinks lower into his seat until at last he lifts his head.

"What?"

"What were you doing at Charlotte's house last night?" I ask, bracing for his answer. "I'm not accusing you of anything!" I begin, as his eyes flash with anger and hurt. "But...you were there. I saw you."

"Yeah, about that." He tilts his head to one side. "Since when are you and Rob house-hunting?"

"House-hunting?" I can't believe what I'm hearing. "We've barely been on one date! I'm pretty sure he's never going to ask me out again. And -" As I stare at my friend the truth of his words slowly starts to click into place. "Charlotte was a realtor."

"That's right." Jeremy turns his cup awkwardly in a circle, scraping it against the countertop. "She was *our* realtor. Mine and Kate's. And that house..." He lets out a shaky breath. "Well, it was going to be a surprise."

"You and Kate were going to get a house together?" I fling my arms around him, and he splutters to be released.

"Well, it isn't going to happen now, is it?" he asks at last. He drains the last of his coffee. "I'm not surprised she was dangling Rob on the line about it too, though. She always was one to drive a hard bargain, and she claimed there were tons of people interested in the place. She was just giving me first refusal because of our past." He rolled his eyes. "Which I'm pretty sure she just made up to make it seem like she was doing me a favor."

"So that's why you were with her last night."

"Yep. And that's what I told Chief Trainor," Jeremy said sharply. "He believed me, I think. Except that, for some reason, he thought I was still dating Charlotte, or still interested in her or something." He shrugged his shoulders. "We broke up ages ago. She has a boyfriend. And I'm with Kate now. I don't know what made him even think..." He trails off, still looking at me and now I know my blush is nice and obvious because I see the hurt in my friend's eyes.

"Is that why you and Rob were following us? Because you thought I was cheating on Kate?"

"Maybe..." I hedge. "But in my defense, I didn't know how serious you guys were. House-hunting! That's big!"

"Yeah, well it's kind of on a back-burner now," he says with a sigh. "Charlotte was the best realtor in town."

"But not the only realtor in town," I say, a memory swimming into focus in my mind. "I bet I know a kid who would happily pull a string or two to get you a discount from someone else eager to make a sale..."

I'm closing up the cafe when my spidey senses start to kick in. I'm not alone. I'm being watched.

I try to focus on my job, pulling the door closed and locking it firmly but instead of dropping my keys back into the pocket of my jacket like I usually would, I wrap my hand carefully around them, lacing them through my fingers so I'm armed with several sharp, pointy objects just in case I need to use them. There's an argument raging in my head. On the one hand, this is Silver Brook, not New York City, but on the other hand...this is Silver Brook. We are now two for two in murders - and that's only the ones that happened recently, and that I know about. *And just because they let Jeremy go doesn't mean they have another viable suspect safely in custody.*

"Merry?"

I yelp and spin around, promptly dropping my keys - my only weapon - onto the ground, where they land with a splash in a puddle.

"Sorry, did I scare you?" Rob steps out of the shadows and reaches down for my keys but I'm quicker, and as I shake off the worst of the water I can't help but feel a flicker of satisfaction that several fat, muddy drops land squarely on his thin cotton scrubs.

"Did you come straight from work?"

"I'm supposed to still be at work." He shoots me a crooked smile and I'm momentarily caught off guard by how cute he looks. Then I remember we aren't exactly on great terms at the moment and I fold my arms and glare at him. He draws a breath, then holds out a bag with a giant gold calligraphy character printed on the side. Mrs. Wu's. I fight the urge to smile but the scent of fresh pad thai reaches my nostrils and makes my stomach growl. You'd think being surrounded by sweet treats all day would kill a girl's appetite, but even though I'm making them and serving them to all and sundry I've not managed to eat very many today.

"We never actually got our meal the other night, so I thought maybe we could try again now." He's so earnest and I'm so hungry that I can feel my reserve weakening and with a groan and turn to unlock the door to the cafe, beckoning him inside.

"We'll go to the kitchen in the back so people don't think the place is still open."

"Good idea." Rob smiles. "I only have like an hour before I need to be back at the surgery. I'm the on-call emergency vet tonight, and I decided to catch up on paperwork." He sighs. "And keep Brick company."

"Brick's still there?" I frown, hitting the lights in the kitchen and pointing him towards a chair. "Is he ok? I thought he'd be back with Emily by now."

Rob places the bag of takeaway down with a thud on the table and stares at me.

"You haven't heard."

"Heard what?" I shrug out of my jacket and bag, dumping them on a spare corner of the table, and start unpacking the food. *Wow, Merry. Is this all it took to get back in your good books?* I remind my conscience that Rob and I hadn't exactly been fighting before this, so my sudden change of heart isn't a sign of weakness, but maturity. *I'm willing to give him the benefit of the doubt. Even if he did almost get one of my best friends arrested for murder.*

"Emily is being held at the police station." He bites his lip, clearly wary of saying more. I remember the way I stormed out of there the last time we saw each other and halt my unpacking progress. That's when his words start to register and a hundred questions start firing around my brain. I struggle with the lid of a pot of jasmine rice.

"Emily is at the police station? Emily Davis? But why? What do they want with her?" I shake my head. "Isn't it enough she's lost her sister?"

"That's kind of the point," Rob says, taking the container of rice out of my hands and opening it easily. He sets it down between us and looks at me. "They found her breaking into Charlotte's house."

"What?!"

"Exactly."

Neither of us moves for a second until I realize the food is getting cold. I grab a couple of clean plates and hand one to him and we start piling them high with noodles, rice, meat, and vegetable dishes, both lost in thought.

"What was she doing there?"

"I have no idea," Rob says, honestly. "But it means that until she's allowed to go home - her own home, I mean - Brick will be staying with me." He smiles, sadly. "I can't take him to my place, not with the menagerie I already have waiting for me, but he's comfortable enough at the clinic, and I'll stay late and go in early to keep him company." He sighs, taking a bite or two of his food. "Poor guy. He's such a sweetheart, even though he does seem to have a habit of hoovering up anything he can find. Even if it's not meant to be eaten."

"Like cufflinks?" I venture.

"Like cufflinks." Rob sighs. "And medical notes. A shoelace. My phone." He pulls it out of his pocket and drops it on the table. I squint at it and can just make out something that looks like toothmarks. "I think he's bored, so I'm going to swing home on my way back and see if I can't liberate a couple of Brodie and Bella's toys to loan him for a while."

"Brodie and Bella?"

"My dogs." Rob smiles, then flips his phone over to show me the lock screen picture. I see him grinning, with his arms around two huge boxers.

"Cute," I say politely, even though I have never been what you might call a dog person. Mind you, I was never a cat person either, until I wound up owning one. My favorite aunt always had dogs I used to like playing with when I visited her as a child, but they were always more toy poodle than trained boxer. I wonder whether I ought to share this story with Rob, but he changes the subject before I get the chance.

"So, Merry. Are we ok?"

"Sure. Why wouldn't we be?" I take a bite of my noodles and allow myself just a moment to enjoy them. This was a perfect interlude in an otherwise hectic day and the last thing I want is to spoil it with a row. "I'm sorry I was a bit off with you earlier," I say, after a moment. "At the police station, I mean. I was worried about my friend."

"And you thought it was my fault he'd been hauled in for questioning."

"No!" I protest, but his eyes are dancing with amusement and I know he sees right through me. "Not exactly."

"I didn't mention him," Rob says, shaking his head for emphasis. "Not a word. I don't know where they pulled his name from but it wasn't me. I swear." He rakes a hand through his hair, and I wonder why I never noticed how attractive that particular gesture could be before now. "I know he's your friend, and he might be cheating on your other friend, but…"

"He isn't!" I bite my lip, then decide there's nothing for it but to tell Rob the truth. "He was using Charlotte to help him buy a house. That's what they were meeting for, that's why they were there. They went to view a house for him and Kate."

"Oh!" Rob catches my eye and laughs. "Well, that's good news then. Good for them." He stops. "I mean…"

"I know." I shake my head. "It's such a mess now. But it means nobody's any closer to figuring out who killed Charlotte." I pause, picking at my food which has suddenly become a lot less appetizing with all this murder talk. "Or why."

"The police seem to think they know," Rob points out, eating a piece of chicken. "They're holding her sister." He winces. "I mean, I have sisters so I know that relationship can be kind of…fraught, at times. As you may have noticed from my ongoing phone argument with one of them on our date." He shakes his head, growing serious at once. "But I don't think I've ever been angry enough at either of them - or anyone else, for that matter - to think of hurting them."

"Maybe Emily was past the point of caring. Charlotte broke her heart when she stole her boyfriend."

"But that was years ago, right?" Rob asks. "Before I moved to Silver Brook, anyway. If she was so angry why wait until now for revenge?"

"Maybe there was something else behind it all…" The food I've eaten settles heavily in my stomach. "Maybe she had more than one reason to hate her sister."

"Or maybe it wasn't her at all," Rob points out, in a manner I think he means to be comforting. "The police were wrong about Jeremy. Maybe they're wrong now, too."

"Maybe." I'm not sure if I want him to be right or not. I don't want Emily to be guilty of killing her own sister. But if it isn't her, then who?

Chapter Eleven

When I roll into work the next morning, Gabe is nowhere to be found. He doesn't show up for the longest time and I'm just starting to get a little worried when he bursts through the front door at the same time as our first few customers of the day.

"You're late!" I call, keeping my voice light so he knows I'm only teasing him. "Did you sleep through your alarm?"

"Something like that." He isn't his usual cheery self and I wonder if he slept at all, he has such large shadows under his eyes.

I ring up a few orders for the eager early customers and once we hit a lull I slip back into the kitchen to find Gabe tapping furiously into his phone. My arrival startles him and he shoves his handset into the back pocket of his jeans before spinning around to meet me with a wide, fake smile.

"What's going on?" I ask, unable to miss the way his hands shake as he fumbles with his apron strings. "Here, let me." I nudge him aside and tie a quick bow, then ask again. "What's up, Gabe? You don't seem like yourself today. Are you sick?" I resist the urge to lay a motherly hand on his forehead to check his temperature. He isn't *that* much younger than me. Besides, he already has a mom. "Want me to call someone?"

"I'm fine," he mutters, shoving past me back into the cafe.

I don't have the mental energy to deal with a teenager and his moods, so I leave him to cover the front of the store while I re-order the kitchen and start a few fresh cookies baking ready for the mid-morning snack rush. I've sort of found my rhythm over the last few days, murder investigation aside, and I'm almost going to miss giving up this place when Maggie comes back to claim it. Maybe I'll see if she can't keep me on. *I'm going to need to find something*, I remind myself. Bouncing from job to job is one thing in your late teens and twenties, but I'm well into my thirties and I need to find some direction, or at least a job that pays enough to keep Snuffy in gourmet pet treats.

Thinking of Snuffy makes me think of Brick and I wonder if he's still trapped at the veterinary surgery with only Rob for company. Not that that's such a bad prospect. I smile to myself, remembering the evening we spent sitting around this very table eating and talking and enjoying a semi-unplanned date. I'm glad we were able to clear the air, and I'm even more glad that he wasn't the one responsible for getting Jeremy in trouble. I think of Emily, embroiled in her own sister's murder, and wonder which of her friends - if any - are going to bat for her. I was so convinced of Jeremy's innocence I would have made up an alibi for him if I'd had to. But Emily?

She was arrested in the middle of committing a crime, I remind myself. *She broke into her sister's house*. From what Rob had said - and I still haven't figured out how he knew it, but I'd place bets on it being his busy-body receptionists - she was very upset when the police arrived and claimed she was only climbing in through the window because she'd lost her spare key. She was looking for something important but hadn't said what. It was suspicious enough for the police to haul her in, anyway, and the fact that she hadn't been seen since made the whole thing sound a lot more serious than it could have been at first glance. *But does that mean she's responsible for murder?* I shudder, wondering what could drive a person to kill their own sister. My breath catches as I remember something that undermines any idea I can have about Emily's responsibility for Charlotte's death. *She hates guns.* So much so that she protested against Rigg's shooting range extending its hours. I remember, now, having to run past her one-person picket line to get to work on time back in the day. *Maybe she changed her mind?* I frown, considering this. *Or maybe someone else was responsible all along.* I think of Mrs. Matthews anxiously reclaiming her gun from Kate and over-explaining why she needed it. *For protection.* I'd thought she meant her own protection, but what if she actually needed it to protect her business? *By taking out the competition?*

I'm still puzzling it out when I hear Gabe's voice rise in pitch and volume through the door. He's talking to one of our customers, I think, but whatever they are arguing about is only getting him more and more agitated. I sprint back into the cafe, ready to insist on him taking a break or going back home to rest but what I see pins my feet to the floor. Gabe's upset, alright. And he's waving around a gun. The same gun his mom said was hers.

• • • •

HE HASN'T SEEN ME. I don't think he really sees anyone. He's crying - huge gasping sobs that make it hard to understand what he's saying.

"She didn't do it. Chief Trainor needs to know that. She didn't hurt anyone. It was - it was me."

"What was you?"

It's Kate who's talking to him, and I wonder how she manages to remain so calm at a time like this.

"All of it!" Gabe gestures with the hand that's holding the gun and I hear a few muffled gasps from other customers who are all hunched low in their seats, watching the drama play out. "My mom didn't know anything! She tried to get me to come forward but I told her she was imagining things. It's - it's me you want, not her."

"Gabe?" I've taken advantage of his focus on Kate to step forward and if she's noticed me she doesn't show it. At the sound of my voice, he spins around and I flinch as I find the gun pointed directly at me. "What's going on?" I try to keep my voice low, the same tone I heard Rob use to calm Snuffy down but it's even less effective now.

"They arrested my mom!" Gabe's eyes flash angrily now, and I realize he isn't crying anymore.

"We've just taken her in for questioning," Kate says, meeting my gaze from behind him. "She said she had an alibi for the night Charlotte was attacked."

"Yeah, she was traveling! She's always traveling. Charlotte stole all her local clients so she has to go further and further out of town to try and make a sale." He shakes his head. "It's not right. She's a good realtor and she's been doing it a lot longer than Charlotte Davis." His lips curl as he spits out her name and I see a flicker of hatred in his eyes that makes me rethink my doubts about him just being a scared kid. "How long until she burns through this job too? She doesn't care if she grinds my mom's career into the dirt before she moves on to her next thing."

"She *didn't* care," Kate corrects him, and he turns his head to look at her, but not before I catch the gleam of a smile on his face.

I can't even believe what happens next. Something about Gabe smiling at the fact that Charlotte Davis is no longer with us - or the fact that I'd been all ready to give the kid the benefit of the doubt - flashes through my limbs like electricity and I take advantage of the fact that he's distracted. I reach for the gun in his hand, jerking it out of his relaxed grip so fast and so sharp that he barely has time to react.

"Hey!"

I'm stunned I was able to take the gun off him so easily, but he seems even more surprised that I tried it. I shake my head, sliding the safety catch onto the gun like I've done it a hundred times before - which I *have* - then dump it into an empty canister of coffee beans, where nobody is going to immediately reach for it.

"You can't just go around shooting people, Gabe."

"She's not wrong," Kate says, fighting a smile as she grabs Gabe and turns him around, leaning across the counter to slap a pair of cuffs on him and start reciting his rights.

The door to the cafe swings open and I see Chief Trainor stride in, ready to take Gabe off Kate's hands and claim the arrest as his idea. I hand Kate the gun, and it's only then that I notice my hands are shaking.

"Good work, Merry," my friend says, with a wink. "You see? All those long hours at the shooting range came in handy. Maybe there'll be a career for you in law enforcement after all!"

"No thank you!" I say, only now realizing just how badly things could have gone a minute earlier. I'd seen Gabe's hold on the gun was loose, but reaching for it could have ended in disaster. People can be unpredictable.

I take a breath and my eyes fall on the last of my current batch of pick-me-up peanut butter cookies. I break off a piece and slip it into my mouth, chewing carefully and allowing the familiar sweet, nutty flavor to soothe my frazzled nerves. Kate and the police chief manage to manhandle Gabe out of the cafe and into the street and I let out a breath and keep eating, breaking crumbs off the cookie and shoveling them into my mouth until it's gone. I'm just thinking about making some more when the door swings open again and a familiar figure hurries toward the counter.

"Hey, Merry, I just heard what happened. Are you ok?" It's Rob, and his handsome features are twisted with concern. Even though I nod, he doesn't seem convinced, because he slides around the side of the counter and is standing right next to me before I have time to lecture him about staff-only spaces and food safety.

"I'm fine," I say, but I'm certainly not going to object when he takes my hand and lays two fingers against my wrist to check my pulse. He smiles at me, then brushes my hair out of my eyes before leaning forward to brush a kiss against my lips. I'm so shocked that I barely register that Rob kissed me - our first kiss! And I wasn't even ready for it! - and when it's over he grimaces. My heart lurches, but that's more to do with his reaction to kissing me than the whole disarming-a-murderer thing. "What?" I ask, not wanting to know the answer. He gives me it anyway, fighting a laugh as he brushes the back of his hand against his lips.

"Have you been eating peanut butter? I hate that stuff!"

Chapter Twelve

I'm in no position to keep the cafe open, and I can only imagine the line of complaints I'll get from my regulars for the decision to close it, but as I turn the key in the lock I know it's the right one.

"So, Mrs. Wu's again?" Rob asks. He hasn't left my side all day and I'm grateful. I'm not sold on the idea of Thai food though. My stomach is still churning after the morning's adventures and I'm not sure I'll be able to keep anything down for hours yet. He seems to guess where my mind has gone because he clarifies. "Just for something to drink. Jasmine tea?"

I wrinkle my nose but agree. I'm pretty sure Mrs. Wu does soda too, for that truly American fusion experience.

We don't make it as far as that before we catch sight of Emily Davis, emerging bleary-eyed from the police department. She catches sight of us and heads straight for Rob, I presume to ask him how Brick is doing. Instead, she throws her arms around *me*!

"Thank you! Oh, thank you, Merry! If you hadn't discovered what happened I don't know how I would have got out of there. They thought that I hurt my sister!" She sniffs back tears. "We didn't get on, Charlotte and I, but I would never...I could never...I don't even own a gun!"

"Neither does Mrs. Matthews," a low voice says to my right, and when I turn my head I notice Jeremy has joined us. He has his *I have news to impart* look on his face, which probably means he's got the scoop from Kate, filtered through her police officer's brain, and is eager to fill me in on all the parts of the story I'm missing. Which is basically all of it.

"We were just heading to Mrs. Wu's for a drink. Do you want to join us?"

"Oh, I…" Emily's looking past me now, her eyes on Rob, and he lays a light hand on my shoulder.

"You guys go on ahead. I have someone at the clinic who is about as keen to see Emily as she is to see him."

"Thank you!" Emily says again, offering me a teary smile and a wave before she falls into step with Rob. I'm smiling too as I watch them leave, thinking of Brick and how happy he will be to have his owner back again.

"Well, hasn't this all worked out well for some of us?" Jeremy asks, offering me his arm in an exaggerated show of gallantry that makes me glare at him before accepting it. I don't feel all that steady on my feet after the day's excitement, although I'm not about to tell him that.

"Somebody died, Jeremy," I remind him. My heart sinks, and my voice drops with it. "And somebody killed her. Somebody I know. A kid!"

"I know." Jeremy is solemn and silent for a moment, then another moment, and in the end I look at him. He's got this strange, faraway look on his face and I nudge him lightly in the side.

"Come on. What did you want to tell me? We can agree it's a tragedy on all sides."

"Just that this seems to have brought you and Rob closer together." He frowns at me. "Although I'm not happy that it took spying on me to do it."

"Spying on you very nearly broke us up before we even got started." I shudder, remembering how I insisted on following

Charlotte to her doom. "I still don't understand why Gabe killed her."

"Money." Jeremy shrugged. "People will do all sorts of crazy things for money."

"No," I say. "I don't think it was that. He genuinely thought he was helping his mom out. Charlotte ruined his mom's business, and it wasn't even like she was in it for the long haul." I bite my lip, remembering the way Gabe had sneered at Charlotte's unhappy habit of jumping from job to job and relationship to relationship. "I don't think she meant to be so heartless."

Jeremy stops and lets out a sigh as he looks at me.

"Meredith Gray. Just because you care too much about other people..." He shakes his head. "Charlotte didn't deserve things to end up the way they did. But she wasn't exactly innocent in all this. She knew Mrs. Matthews was the only other realtor in town and she was determined to steal her business. Why do you think she was giving people deals and snapping up clients before her competition even got the chance to? She had a lot of contacts in this town and she was using every single one of them to make her business a success while Gabe's mom's failed."

"And now neither of them can work." I shake my head, thinking of poor Mrs. Matthews, embroiled in this mess because she tried to cover for her son.

We walk on in silence and it's only when we reach Mrs. Wu's that I remember another wrinkle in the story that doesn't make any sense.

"Why did Mrs. Matthews have a gun if she didn't own one?"

Jeremy shakes his head a second time, then fits the final piece of the puzzle together for me.

"It wasn't hers. Mrs. Matthews found the gun in Gabe's bag. When they were rowing at the cafe the other day it was because she'd come to confront him about it. She wanted to march straight over to the police station and hand it in, but he begged her not to. He promised her he wasn't using it but spun some story about violence at work - here, if you can believe it - saying he'd just brought it for protection. Just in case. She was covering for him, but she didn't realize what she was covering for him for. Word was the police were starting to look at her, thanks to my intrepid girlfriend the detective putting two and two together about the suspicious gun possession. That's when everything seems to have come crashing down for Gabe. He couldn't let his mom get in trouble for his crime." Jeremy's voice hardens. "Although it appears he didn't feel the same way about me, or about Emily."

"He's just a kid," I remind him, gently.

"Who killed someone." Jeremy sighs. "Anyway, that's the story as much as I can piece it together. Only, don't spread it around just yet, alright? Kate told me and I kind of promised her I wouldn't tell anyone else." He raises his eyebrows at me and I mime zipping my lips shut. We find a free table and a harried-looking Mrs. Wu dashes towards us, flapping her hands at me in a panic.

"I just heard, Meredith! Gabriel is a murderer! Gabriel who works here! All this time, I had a murderer right under the roof and I never knew!"

I bite my lip, deciding now isn't the best time to remind her that this is the second murder we've had in Silver Brook, and the last perpetrator was probably a regular here too.

"And you!" Mrs. Wu throws her arms around me in an elbowy hug. "He tried to hurt you!"

"He didn't! Not really," I reassure her, patting her awkwardly on the back. "I don't even think he meant to hurt anyone. Things just got out of hand." I smile hoping Mrs. Wu can't see through this small fib. I can't quite forget the sly smile on Gabe's face and wonder if he only meant to scare Charlotte off, or... I don't suppose we'll ever really know the truth.

"That doesn't make it right!" Mrs. Wu sighs. "And now I have to find a new waiter!" Her eyes narrow as she looks at me as if it's my fault that Gabe will no longer be available to work the graveyard shift for her.

"Well, me too," I remind her. "Maggie's going to come back to a just-about-functioning cafe and only half the staff she left with." I see several other customers waving their hands to attract Mrs. Wu's attention and before she dashes off to serve them I manage to order two sodas for Jeremy and me. He smiles at me across the table and I find myself smiling tiredly back.

"So, are you going to tell Maggie what happened at the Jitterbug Junction or play it down?" Jeremy shoots me a look. "Getting over a murder was the whole reason for her impromptu getaway, wasn't it? Not exactly the welcome back to Silver Brook she'll be expecting, or wanting."

"Right." I frown. I need to come up with something to overshadow this latest bout of bad news. "She deserves a better welcome back than that. And I need to prove that, despite everything, she picked the right person to run her cafe."

The day Maggie Pritchard is due back in Silver Brook dawns bright and sunny, but I barely notice. It was still dark when I got up, and I've been hard at work ever since.

"Where do you want the banner, Merry?" Kate asks, through a yawn. "In the window?" She's holding onto one corner, but the rest of it is draped over Jeremy, who is struggling to keep it off the floor. They move towards the window but I stop them halfway there.

"No, put it on this wall." I point in the opposite direction. "That way Maggie will see it as soon as she walks in."

"Good plan." Kate beams at me. "You have an eye for this stuff."

"Last minute party prep?"

"What looks good where. Staging. This whole thing."

I frown but let the comment slide. Kate has been extra nice to me lately. I think she's worried my life is going to fall apart once Maggie comes back and reclaims her cafe. I'll confess, it's certainly a thought I've had once or twice. Just what am I going to do with myself once I'm not needed here?

"I have flowers!" Rob appears from the kitchen holding a surprising number of vases with bouquets in them. He stifles a sneeze. "Someone take them off me before my allergies really get triggered."

"Allergies?" I ask, helping him out by sliding two vases free and placing them down on the tables nearest us.

"P-p-pollen." He says, holding his breath to keep from sneezing. "And peanuts." He winks. "But that's more of a

personal hatred than this-product-is-actively-trying-to-kill-me."
He sneezes. "Flowers, on the other hand..."

"Well, here, let me help you." We follow each other around
the cafe, dotting vases of flowers on empty tables and I survey
the room. I decided to bring a little bit of sparkle to the cafe to
welcome Maggie back in style. All it took was rearranging some
furniture and adding a few new touches - like the flowers Rob is
now scowling at while he sniffs back more sneezes - but it's given
the cafe a whole new look.

"Does this count as a date?" he asks, abandoning all
pretences and reaching for a handkerchief. "That makes three, by
my count."

"Three?"

"Our first attempt at Mrs. Wu's - which began and ended our
spying career." He glances over his shoulder to ensure Jeremy and
Kate are out of earshot and I swallow past a lump in my throat,
wishing I could forget that whole dreadful evening but knowing
it'll take a long time before I can. "Our second attempt at Mrs.
Wu's," Rob continues. "When I brought takeaway and we ate it
in that very cozy little kitchen over there." He blew noisily into
his handkerchief. "And now. This makes three."

"I guess it does." I'm fighting a smile. He even manages to
look cute now, when he's all blotchy and watery-eyed.

"So, what I'm wondering is, when are we going to make it
official?"

"Make what official?" Jeremy's supersonic hearing has kicked
in again and he zeroes in on us, marching over to where we are
standing.

"Nothing." I shake my head, but Rob isn't so easily deterred. He slings an arm around my shoulders and even I can't deny how comfortable it feels.

"Merry and I are a couple." He grins at me. "Officially."

"About time!" Kate calls, as she steps back to survey their sign with a critical eye. "Jeremy and I were worried we were going to have to stage a proper intervention to get you to admit you liked each other..."

"Admit who likes each other?"

The door to the cafe swings open and Maggie herself strides in, a full hour before she's due to arrive.

"Maggie!"

"Welcome home!"

"What is this?" she laughs, greeting us all with hugs and smiles, and looks around us at the changes to the Jitterbug's interior. "What's going on?"

"We're throwing you a welcome home party!" I say, pointing to the sign. "Only, you're a little early."

"Not too early for cookies!" Jeremy exclaims, brandishing a plate piled high with chocolate chip, shortbread, and my famous peanut butter cookies, which Maggie obediently tries.

"These are amazing! Did you make them?"

"She certainly did." Rob gives a feigned shudder and I make a show of selecting a plain and peanut-free shortbread before breaking it in half for us to share.

"Well, Merry! You certainly seem to have managed to run the place pretty well without me." Maggie's eyes are dancing and I feel like she's about to tell us all something big. "Which is good news. Because I'm only here for a flying visit. Just long enough to tie things up here and get back on the road. I've had an offer of a job in a new town and I think I'm going to take it."

"You're leaving?" Jeremy looks at me. "But what about this place?"

"Well, that's just it. I was worrying about what to do about it, but now I see I don't have to. I've got the perfect manager right here." She turns to me, her eyes bright. "What do you say, Merry? Do you want to take this place on full-time?"

I think of how focused and fulfilled I've felt the last few weeks - new romance and murder investigation aside - and give the only answer I could ever dream of.

"I thought you'd never ask!"

The End

About the Author

When Rachel Beattie isn't writing stories, she's usually reading them - especially of the cozy mystery variety. A lifelong devotee of Agatha Christie, she loves putting ze little grey cells to work and is especially fond of anything that can make her laugh while she's collecting a clue or two.

• • • •

Join her mailing list[1] for more information, new release news, exclusives and bonus content.

---

1. https://mailchi.mp/003ddbbcc668/newsletter-subscribers

Also by Rachel Beattie

A Serenity Suites Cozy Mystery
Cassie Clinton and the First Fatality
Double Trouble for Cassie Clinton
Cassie Clinton and the Triple Threat

A Slice of Life Cozy Mystery
Love, Lies and Pumpkin Spice
Wed, Dead and Gingerbread
Crime Scenes and Blackcurrant Cream
Spirits, Spells and Caramel
Broken Hearts and Strawberry Tarts
Black Tie and Vanilla Pie
A Slice of Life Cozy Mystery Books 1-3

A Very Merry Murder Mystery
The Santa Slaughter
The First Date Disaster
The Body in the Bookstore

The Harmony Inn Homicide
The Scandal at the Spa
The Babysitter Bungle
The Campground Killer
The Deadly Dinner Party
The Flower Shop Felony
A Very Merry Murder Mystery Books 1-3

www.ingramcontent.com/pod-product-compliance
Lightning Source LLC
Chambersburg PA
CBHW051247160726
47994CB00003B/1058